Decline and Fall of Rowland Graves

by Eris Adderly

This book is a work of fiction. Names, characters, places, and incidents either are products of the author's imagination or are used fictitiously. Any resemblance to actual persons, living or dead, events, or locales is entirely coincidental.

THE DECLINE AND FALL OF ROWLAND GRAVES

Copyright © 2015-2016 Eris Adderly

All Rights Reserved

No part of this book may be reproduced in any form or by any electronic or mechanical means including information storage and retrieval systems, without permission in writing from the author. The only exception is by a reviewer, who may quote short excerpts in a review.

First eBook Edition: October 2015
Kindle Edition

Cover Design by Eris Adderly.

Acknowledgements

Thank you to my husband for more than one night of sitting down and debating this plot to death. Thank you Mister Jim for helping me weed out those pesky Americanisms and everything else that caught your careful eye. Thank you to Nora who really pumped me up about this dark horse of a story, and for loving Judith, who probably needed it more than anyone else. And thank you to all the dead people who look the other way when I write silly things. You know I love you.

Contents

Promises, Light and Dark	7
A Terrible Perseverance	17
Paved With Good Intentions	31
The Dove and the Fox	51
Descent	67
The One	79

I

Promises, Light and Dark

"I was never really insane except upon occasions when my heart was touched."
— Edgar Allan Poe

Bristol, England, 1692

Pale lashes fluttered their downy kisses over cheeks of blushing ivory. The cool light of an October afternoon made purple shadows play in the well at the base of a throat. Her throat.

His angel.

Her breath hitched again and the golden brow tightened into a delicate furrow in time with the skilful movements of his hand between their bodies. The house was empty save for they two; the tufted chaise near the tall window in her bedroom a perfect bed for her sighs.

"Rowland …"

He smiled to himself and ignored her, his teeth nipping at her neckline, teasing one of the spring-pink buds out into the open. When she whispered his name it was a seraph anointing him, and he'd hear it again before relenting.

Drawing the dainty perking tip into his mouth in a careful suckling, Rowland circled his free hand tighter at her waist, pulling her closer. Yards and yards of taffeta, the palest yellow, piled in rustling bunches over her hips. One silk-smooth thigh, the colour of fresh milk, lay draped over each of his while his splayed hand at her waist was all that kept her from falling back against the chaise.

He rolled at the little bead of pleasure with his fingers, the pearl he knew would release those pretty sounds from her lips, and slid a second finger now into her warmth. She whimpered at his touch and his heart soared. Whatever he could discover to make this perfect creature happy, he would do.

Her hands were at his shoulders, threading through his hair. Of their own accord, her hips sought closer contact, so innocently answering his call to sensation.

"Rowland, please ..."

There was nothing more exquisite than his own name on her lips.

"Yes, love?"

"Please, I ..." His fingers twitched and her plea fragmented into a quiet gasp.

"What is it you want, Little Dove?" he asked, his voice a gentle taunt. It was rapture when she came unfocused at his touch, and Rowland continued plucking the lovely notes from her as though she were the finest harp, made to sing only for him.

"I ... I ... Please! You know what I want!" Her breathy desperation had him grasping for his own self-control now, but he was intent on drawing out her beautiful torment for a time longer.

"I know," he said, pushing the fabric of her skirts higher still, "I know what you want. But not yet, love."

He slid his own body down the chaise then, out from under her parted thighs, until his face was level with the dewy lips he'd just been exploring with his hand. She was heaven to inhale; tangy and sweet, and he slid a palm under her bottom to bring her closer.

His angel wanted them to be together, and this he wanted also, but he would taste her first and hear her come undone before he allowed himself to fall apart in the joy of her embrace.

The first lap at her honeyed furrow brought a gasp and a soft moan of release. It seemed today she'd forget her shame and let him do this: let him paint her with gleaming strokes of worship again.

Warm, wet flesh smothered his mouth, his nose. His tongue plunged and rasped, finding the places that made her chirp her approval. He brought his fingers back, parting her for a more thorough consumption. When he slid them inside her again, though, her low groan was the first unladylike thing he'd heard that afternoon.

Lovely.

She was losing control.

He set his mouth in a gentle suction over that eager pink button of hers and drew her in to match the rhythm of his stroking fingers. Her hips bucked at him and she cried out.

Yes, Angel.

His tempo became more deliberate: fingertips curling and beckoning her towards surrender along with the insistent pulling plea from his lips. Closer now. Closer...

A breathy crescendo of clipped moans blurred into a wail of release. Her body clutched at his fingers, hips rising away from the chaise. He felt her walls fluttering against him: a song. A promise.

"Rowland ..." She sighed, the tension in her limbs floating away.

He could wait no longer.

A man had never pushed aside a pair of breeches so fast. He needed her. Kneeling between her thighs again, he hauled her up into his lap, sliding the heat of his arousal along the wet mess he'd brought about with his tongue. He bent double over her, catching her swollen lips in a kiss.

"Is this what you want, Dove?" He spoke the urgent words against her mouth. He would always ask permission, no matter how many times she'd given it in the past.

"Yes!" She arched against him. "Oh yes, *please!*"

With a push, he was inside her. His arms circled her waist and he sat back up, bringing her upright with him. For a moment, he did nothing; simply held her there, sheathed in her heat, her love. Something inside her flexed, grasped at him. He hissed.

"Elinor."

Her eyes held his, the palest blue, and her thumb smoothed over his cheekbone. The fabric of her bodice slid under his palms as he pressed the two of them closer. He wanted to thrust into her like a beast, but not as much as he wanted to watch her pluck up the courage herself.

Their lips were together again, tongues affectionate, questing. Then … it happened.

She began to move.

First a shy turn of hips that gripped at his heart, but then a more deliberate roll. He gritted his teeth, trying to be still, allowing her to find her way. The rolling became a grind. Her legs were about him now as she pressed him as far inside as he would go.

With a final, almost chaste kiss for him, he felt her abandon restraint. She rose up, clenching her muscles to lift herself nearly all the way off, before falling onto him again, burying his length to the hilt. It was Rowland's turn to groan.

His Elinor took up the dance then in earnest, the rising away and then dropping back, slamming her confession against him with each maddening jerk of her hips.

"Love." It was all he could do to grind out the word. Each dull slap of her body against him sent jarring blows of pleasure straight up his spine.

"Yes, Rowland?" Her voice was breathy, bouncing out over her own movements.

"I need ..." His breath came short, words hoarse. "I need to ..."

"I know, Love. Take it. Please."

She knew. Knew he was going mad to keep still this way, and was ready to help end his torment.

In a single move, he had her cradled back against the chaise, his body covering hers. Those eyes ... those eyes denying him nothing. He plunged home with a primal noise of satisfaction, and she opened wider, giving of herself. He took.

His hips worked into her with a frenzy, joining them again and again as though there would be no time tomorrow for such boundless delight. Sounds of lust and encouragement forced their way out under his pounding now, and she called out his name in time with their coupling.

I can't go on like this! I can't—

She tilted her hips just so and Rowland lost his hold on reality.

"Elinor!"

He drove in with a final roar of completion, seating himself to the limits of her depth and spilling out his love with pulse after pulse of blinding joy.

His eyes were clenched shut and his ears rang, but after an immeasurable time, the fog cleared and he sank back down to the chaise. To his angel.

She smiled up at him, fingertips dusting over his chest, and he twitched within her, his body still shuddering to a stop.

"I love you, Rowland."

He wanted to collapse every time he heard the words.

"And I love *you*," he replied as he always did, brushing her lips in a kiss.

Their clothing righted again a few moments later, he pulled her back onto his lap and drew his arms around her waist.

"We'll tell your father on Friday, yes?" He nuzzled his face into her neck.

"Mmm. Yes," she said, curling around his needy affection in welcome. "I can't bear to wait any longer. We'll wed in the spring, Love?"

"Of course," he said, threading his fingers through hers, bringing her knuckles to his lips.

How or why Fortune had chosen to favour him, he wasn't sure, but he at least knew one thing. Elinor Barlow loved him. Beyond all reason, Rowland Graves had earned the love of an angel, and his every day and night with her would be a blessing. He would adore her and hold her every one of them.

Judith Barlow stood again, taking a silent step away from her younger sister's bedroom door, the lines of her face hardening. Such a tiny opening to cause her to see such an immense truth.

A mere keyhole, a furtive whimper, and her walking past just at that time, on her way to her own room to retrieve a forgotten scarf. When the sound on the other side of the door had stopped her mid-step, her first instinct had been to whip open the door and see to her sister's well-being. Another step towards the bedroom, however, and the noise rang clear, if quiet, as something other than pain.

It can't be.

She'd slid out of her slippers and moved the rest of the way to the door, bending to lower an eye to the keyhole. Now she was no longer certain whether this had been a good idea.

Her lip turned in disgust.

Rowland Graves. Spreading my sister out like some whore. Have they both lost their minds?

He was blind if he thought Elinor the sort of young woman meant to be with someone like him. And she, mad, if she thought because she was the perfect daughter, the innocent one, that Father would ever approve of such a thing. That silly girl didn't know what love *was*. The final words she'd heard about a wedding ...

Their father would hear about this. Oh, yes.

Backing into her slippers again with silent feet, Judith stole down the hall and back to her original mission of collecting her scarf, her aim in meeting her father this afternoon appended. This business would end, and end tonight.

"Mr Dunning, will you please escort the gentlemen into the dining room?"

The women had already filed into the dining hall in a rustling of silks and taffeta, and now the men were moving in behind them, once Abraham Barlow had asked his guest to lead them. Rowland didn't know this Mr Dunning, but Barlow had been doing a fine job of bending his ear while the guests had gathered in the drawing room to converse before dinner.

They entered and took seats according to status. Rowland found himself sitting one chair from the end of the men's side of the table, furthest away from Mr Barlow. It came as no surprise—the men between him and the master of the house were a sampling of his business partners, wealthy financiers, merchants and the like. He didn't know all their names, and didn't particularly care to, either.

Barlow had only invited him due to his role as the family physician, and his seat was so far from the head of the table because he'd only taken over that position a little more than a year ago from his predecessor, who'd retired. Not enough time for him to have built a reputation yet, but just long enough to have fallen helplessly in love with his employer's younger daughter. And by some miraculous blessing from the Lord, she loved him in return.

His eyes sought his angel and found her. Elinor sat one seat removed from her father on the women's side of the table. Only her sister Judith sat closer. Two women could not look more alike and be less similar.

Judith Barlow was older than her sister by a mere two years and, aside from having brown eyes that tilted at a slightly more noticeable angle than Elinor's lovely blues, the two could hardly be told apart. That was, at least, until one heard them speak. Then all confusion vanished.

Where his Elinor was sweet and dainty, Judith was shrewish and biting. One all innocence, the other a thorny bed of schemes and vicious gossip. He pitied whatever poor man that one might set her eye on for marriage, should a creature the likes of her choose out such a victim at all.

Servants were carrying out the first course, and Rowland had to pay attention lest the trays and dishes being set down over the shoulders of guests bump him and spill out their contents. There was hardly room for the vegetables and stews around the garish sugar sculpture that ran the central length of the table. Aphrodite stood at one end, all in white sugar and almond paste, and a fat Cupid at the other. An out-of-character choice for the sober Abraham Barlow, but perhaps it had been the confectioner's doing.

Still, he had eyes almost entirely for Elinor as the meal wore on—what seemed like forever as these affairs were wont to do—with the occasional glance at her father to assess whether the time was right for him to fling his fate to the gods and announce his intentions. How could the man say no? Rowland was a *doctor*, for heaven's sake. What more suitable husband could a man want for his daughter?

The way his Dove handled her knife, the delicate touch of her fingers around the stem of her glass, her musical laugh, like little bells tinkling ... He was overcome with love for her and the longer the meal wore on, the more insistent became the thundering heart in his chest. He knew he must say something soon, or run out of time.

By the last course, dessert, he was nearly shaking in his seat. This was not like his normal controlled surety, but then he had never asked a man for his daughter's hand before today.

Even though the dessert course offered guests the opportunity to reseat themselves according to pleasure rather than status, no one had moved.

They're probably too bloated and full to want to bother with standing up.

This left Rowland still at the far end of the table, and it was clear he would have no choice but to stand up and be loud about it.

Now, Rowland. Do it now, before you lose your nerve.

His eyes flitted to Elinor, who gave him the shyest of smiles before she looked back down at the table. She knew he was ready.

He stood, pushing his chair back as he rose, mouth open to address Abraham Barlow.

Abraham Barlow was coming to his feet as well.

What's this?

The man was clearly about to speak himself, but Rowland had caught his eye. Barlow made a slightly bothered face in his direction and adjusted his coat with a mild tug.

"Just a moment, Doctor Graves," he said. "I have some news I'd like to share, and then I'm sure we'll be more than happy to hear whatever it is you have for us this evening."

Rowland gave a small nod and resumed his seat. At least the man had acknowledged him. He only hoped it wouldn't be a long speech from Barlow so his courage wouldn't have time to wane.

"My friends," Barlow began, laying a hand on the shoulder of the man to his right, who stood at the prompt as though he was already privy to the coming information, "most of you are familiar with Mr Walter Dunning, if not personally, then by his impressive reputation ..."

I've *never heard of him.*

Barlow prattled on about Dunning's achievements and status, and Rowland waited for the man to have done with revealing whatever self-congratulatory business deal the two of them had arranged so he could state his own intentions.

"And so it is with great pleasure"—the man seemed to be finally putting a cap on it—"that I announce the engagement of Mr Dunning—"

Oh dear Lord.

He'd seen Judith grinning that prickly secretive grin of hers all night.

That poor, poor man.

"— to my youngest daughter, Elinor."

Rowland blinked. Twice. His lower internal organs seemed to be ... gone. He was rooted to his chair and his throat felt hollow.

What?

Elinor's eyes were saucers, her lips parted. She stared at her father.

What did he just say?

The rest of the room was erupting with applause and cheers and back slapping. His angel turned her wide blue eyes in his direction, giving him a discreet, bewildered shake of her head.

Engaged to ... Elinor? His Elinor?

The shrew sister dabbed at the corner of her smirking mouth with a napkin.

His face was growing hot, and the jovial congratulations breaking all around him seemed to dull under the rushing of blood in his ears. Rowland barely heard Abraham Barlow saying his name as he stood to take himself away from the dining room as quickly as he could get his legs to obey.

"What was it you wanted to say now, Doctor Graves? Doctor Graves?"

II

A Terrible Perseverance

"Rowland you have to calm yourself! How could I have had any idea?"

The seldom-used guest bedroom was lit only by an opening between narrowly parted drapes and the white hot anger shimmering in the air around Rowland Graves.

"Your sister certainly seemed to know something!" he said, gesturing wildly in the dark.

"I don't know how she could have found out, Love!" Elinor pled, ignoring the nimbus of danger rolling off of him to stand close, her dainty hands coming to the lapels of his coat.

He could smell her light perfume, feel her wrists nearly trembling against him, and was overcome with shame. It was time to get himself under control. Rowland couldn't hiss and spew venom this way in the presence of his little dove; she didn't deserve it.

"I'm sorry, Angel," he schooled his voice into a semblance of composure and circled her shoulders with his arms, pulling her close. "It isn't your fault. I'm only upset at what has happened, not at you."

His apologies were spoken low against the silken cloud of her hair, and his hands stroked at the tresses, at her neck and shoulders. The very presence of Elinor Barlow was a soothing bastion to which he could cling, could maintain his sanity at a time like this. She was a balm to keep his jagged edges smooth. He'd come to need her so very badly.

"I ... I simply think I *hate* her sometimes, Rowland!" She sniffled against his collar. "I know! I *know* I should never say something so wicked, but ... but it seems she *wants* me to be unhappy! She *must* have said something to Father! Why, Love? Why has this happened to us?"

Her sobbing was spiralling out of control now, and it appeared to be his turn to calm *her*. It wouldn't do for someone to discover them alone together this way, and that was just what would happen if they weren't quiet.

"Shh, Elinor. Please." He lowered his voice, hoping to prompt her to do the same, and drew partway out of their embrace to look down into her eyes. They gleamed wetly in the moonlight from the window. "We'll figure out a way, Dove." He attempted to reassure her—reassure them both, truth be told—and tilted his face to brush his lips over her forehead at her hairline.

"The wedding isn't until next year." He said the word with disgust now that it meant someone other than himself marrying Elinor. "Perhaps you can speak to your father? Convince him you don't wish to marry Dunning?"

She looked up at him then, as though the idea had never occurred to her.

"Yes. Yes, of course I will!" He watched a whisper of a smile return to her face in the dim light. "Father is reasonable, Rowland. He *must* listen to me! He would never want me to be unhappy."

Watching hope fill her up again, hidden away as they were in this quiet, remote corner of the house, made something stir within him, as well. He lowered his face and brought his mouth against hers. The tiny whimper of expectation he received in response nearly buckled his knees.

Yes, how could anyone ever want you to be unhappy?

She parted for him, offering up the slightest tease of her tongue, just as she knew he liked to be baited into pursuit. He chased her back into her own mouth, tasting and nipping.

Perfect. So Perfect.

In the midst of perfection, though, some dark thing twitched and coiled at the base of his spine. His pull at her mouth became more insistent.

We'd better rectify this situation, hadn't we, Graves? We'd bloody well better or else …

A low growl rumbled up from somewhere deep in his throat and he realised he was backing her towards a low dresser that stood against the wall between two windows. When her backside came against its edge, the increased demands of his kisses muffled her startled gasp.

"Rowland …" Her voice had a disoriented edge as she pulled away. It was as might be expected; he couldn't remember ever giving into his urges with her this way.

"I can't stand it, Love," he said, taking her face in both his hands.

"What's that?" She looked up at him with wide eyes in the darkness, voice and body tight. "What can't you stand?"

"Dunning! The thought of him even *touching* you!" He leaned in to wrest a further series of bruising kisses from her.

She was breathless when they broke it off. His hands were on either side of her on the dresser now and she bent back at the waist to catch her breath.

"Oh, Rowland! I would never—"

"If your father marries you off to him you'll have to!" It was becoming more and more difficult for him to keep his voice down.

"Please! I will *never*!" Her insistence begged him to believe. "I only belong to you, my love!"

Rowland inhaled through his nose at those words, teeth clenching together under the tightening of his jaw. His hands came together at her waist and caught her up.

"Yes, Elinor," he said, with a low crackling of threat in his tone for anyone who dared take his angel from him. He hoisted her up to sit on the edge of the dresser. "You *do* belong to me."

The ferocity of his next kiss, his handling, startled a clipped moan out of her. Rowland devoured it along with every other beautiful little whimper and gasp that followed.

Her hands were at his shoulders to steady herself, lest she fall back against the wall under his forceful claims. His mouth was on the moving column of her throat, the rising flesh of her breast at her neckline. She accepted him though, rough hands and all. Elinor always accepted him, any way that he came to her. Her knees were pressing in at his hips, and he snarled with some discomfiting new sense of possession.

She belongs to me. Me!

He clawed at skirts and petticoats, gathering endless fabric over her knees. He had to be inside her. To feel her. To know.

She was soaked when he found her with his fingers, and she pulled her lower lip between her teeth to hold back her sounds of want at his touch. His free hand was tugging at his breeches and shirt, shifting them out of the way so his aching, steel-hard need could pour out heat between them. They needed to be joined together. Now.

Ask her, Rowland. You always ask first.

It was all he could do to rasp out the words as he traced his fingers through the moisture between her thighs.

"Is this what you want, Elinor?"

"Yes, Love," she said, "but wait."

"Mmm?" He couldn't even form proper words.

Wait for what?

"Let me," she said, and he felt her soft fingers circling his base in the dark, guiding him.

His Elinor brought him to her own wet entrance and he nearly came unravelled as she nudged the blunt tip where it was meant to go before releasing her hand. She leaned back a fraction of a degree, inviting him to bring them the rest of the way. Rowland didn't need her to ask him twice.

With a slick push he was home, her walls clasping at him in affirmation. He could not go slow, not be gentle on this maddening night. Immediately he was thrusting, ploughing into her. She drew her knees apart wider, telling him with her body that his fierce claims could be acted out this evening without regret.

She accepts the basest side of you, Rowland. You must do everything in your power not to lose her.

His hand was at the back of her neck, his forehead pressed against hers as his hips and thighs worked, delivering his cock over and over into her delicious, clutching heat. He felt her bottom scooting closer to the edge of the dresser, hips tilting, seeking.

Greedy man. Let her enjoy this, too.

He brought his thumb between them, circling the pad amongst the slippery folds just above where he was moving, splitting her in two. His angel felt so impossibly perfect around him, and each time his thumb shifted back and forth across that firm little kernel of pleasure, he felt her grasp at him from inside.

Forcing himself to slow his movements, Rowland concentrated his efforts now on increasing the frequency of her helpless, delicate spasms, delighting in the way they rippled over his flesh.

Her tightly restrained noises of pleasure were increasing in pitch and desperation, and it was all he could do to keep his motions deliberate and not pound into her like a madman.

Then: she was silent. Her body clutched at him in a pronounced series of fluttering contractions. Once. Twice. A third time, and she held him, clenched from within, her head falling back in the darkness, rolled under by her own release.

He leaned in to kiss and lap at her collar bone, tasting the salty thin sheen of sweat there, the movement of his hips taking up its mission in earnest once again.

"Tell me," he said, gripping her at the hips now for leverage.

He heard her swallow, wetting her throat again.

"Tell you what?"

"Tell me you belong to me." The desperate need to hear it when the fact was already so plain was disturbing.

Her hips were sliding further off the dresser.

"No," she said, her voice a low tone he couldn't remember hearing before tonight.

Her legs were coming down now, feet reaching for the floor, and he felt himself dislodged.

"Elinor, what—"

"I don't want to tell you, Rowland," she said, the rasp of desire unmistakable now. His angel had never spoken to him this way. "I want to show you."

She pushed him back with her palms and, baffled, he stepped away, erection standing straight out from his body, demanding to know what had just happened.

"I don't understand, Love," he said with a shake of his head and a small, meaningless gesture of hands.

What is she on about?

"I want to show you that you're the only man I will *ever* belong to," she said, stepping towards him. "That every part of my body and spirit is yours, the way it will be for no other."

He could see her flushed skin and parted lips in the cool light of the moon, and wanted to pull her into a fast embrace at such words, though he still didn't understand.

Elinor gave him no time to do so, however, and sank to her knees in a broad puddle of fabric. Before more questions had time to form on his lips, one of her pale hands was gripping his still eager cock and he watched her lean close.

The light in the room was barely enough for a body to move about by, but he knew her blue eyes were intent on his face from the way her neck was tilted up. There were light, feminine strokes along hot, hard flesh and he balled his hands into fists at his sides, his certainty still tumbling end over end at this bizarre turn of events.

"*Every* part of my body, Rowland ..."

She dipped her head and he felt ...

Rowland gasped.

He felt a warm, soft tongue being drawn along the underside of his cock.

"... even the lips I say my prayers with."

She took him into her mouth, the hot, sweet luxury a contrast to the cool air of the room. He nearly collapsed at the sensation.

And those words. Such sinful words from his perfect angel. They were enough to make a man spill everything he had right on the spot. He fought for control.

Elinor, his innocent dove, was suckling at him now, pulling, doing maddening things with her tongue and teeth.

From where had this come? He had never asked her to indulge him in such an act. Wouldn't have been able to even speak of a thing like this in front of her. Certainly she let him taste *her*, from time to time, but this ... This was different. She ...

She was easing her lips further and further down the length of his shaft. He wished there was more light, couldn't imagine what her lovely face must look like, jaw parted, working. Rowland was straining, losing his grip. He'd need to pull away soon, before he lost himself.

A hand was tugging, kneading at the loose skin of his scrotum now. The tip of her nose came to just brush against his body, and he felt her palate and the back of her throat closing in around him. Subtle shifts of her tongue while all else was still were sending him into lightning-quick flashes of freefall he couldn't control.

No, Rowland. Don't do that to her.

He jerked his hips back.

"Elinor, wait! No! You don't want—"

"Yes. I do."

Her hands were at his hips and, in a single swift move, had him buried to the hilt down her lovely throat.

This is some mad dream! I'll wake in the morning and this entire dinner will have never happened!

She was moving now, bobbing, drawing him in with an eager suction, hands stroking over him in time with the efforts of her mouth. Then came her moans. Feminine, muffled mewling over the impossibly hard girth stretching her lips apart.

Every part of my body, Rowland ...

You're the only man I will ever belong to.

He bit back a roar as white light exploded behind his eyelids. His balls rose up, tightened. The pulsing began and he couldn't stop it.

Every bit of love, frustration, fear, and joy spilled in hot waves down the back of her throat, and she drew from the tap, accepting, swallowing, devouring. Elinor tugged at him still, her small, slick fist milking him for every drop, and he shuddered under her touch until he had to pull away, to stop her when it became too much.

Rowland staggered backwards to the small bed in the room, knees giving out just as he sat back. His angel was on her feet, coming to him, standing between his knees, kissing him before he had a chance to catch his breath.

"I love you, Rowland," she said when they settled, her hands at his shoulders.

"And I love *you*."

The words they said were the same as they'd been for months now, affirmations of love. But the rest?

What world was this? That his quiet little dove could give him such a gift? If this could happen, what else?

Perhaps this was a world now where inconvenient engagements could be broken off, wriggled out of with enough finesse.

Yes.

He and Elinor *would* be together. He was sure of it.

"But Mrs Barlow, that's terrible! Let us go to my grandfather at once! Something must be done!"

"I *cannot* go to him!" Judith grasped the fingers of Margaret Ellery even tighter, and allowed her voice to crack just enough. "Don't you see, Mrs Ellery? That's why I've come to *you*. I cannot have such a shameful thing be known about me, about my sister. What it would do to Father to hear it! Or my sister's fiancé?"

Her voice was a whispered hiss that matched the light breeze along the garden's tall yew hedges, but the chill in the air didn't cool the few hot tears rolling down her cheeks. Thank Heaven this was a secluded area.

"But what can *I* do?" the young woman asked, shaking her pretty amber ringlets in confusion.

Look at her. Can't be more than a day over eighteen. Easy enough to steer in the right direction.

"Go to your grandfather," Judith said, "Tell him what I've told you, only let him know that, for the sake of a family's reputation, the women involved don't wish to have their names mentioned."

Young Mrs Ellery drew her hands towards herself, shoulders slumping, eyes taking a particular interest in a bit of lace on her apron, a look of scepticism furrowing her otherwise smooth brow.

"Please," Judith continued, wondering to herself whether actual hand-wringing might be too much. "If you can only convince him to write a letter."

"A letter to whom?"

"To the Fellows. At Oxford. This can't be allowed to

continue, and perhaps if word is sent from someone they respect, like your grandfather, they can put a stop to it before it goes any further. Before any other women are ... are ..." She punctuated her plea with a few more well-placed tears for full effect, refusing to repeat the scandalous words she'd already planted in Margaret Ellery's ear.

"Oh yes, of course!" the young woman said, bravery welling up as she pulled Judith in for what she likely thought of as a comforting embrace. "Why of *course* he can send a letter. Quite right, Mrs Barlow. I'll tell him this evening, I promise—after dinner—and see that the letter is sent off myself. We'll set things right, you'll see. He'll never be in a position to do it again."

Oh, I suspect that will indeed *be the case, Mrs Ellery.*

After much clasping of hands and further sniffling reassurances, Judith was able to shed herself of the earnest Margaret Ellery and make her way back through the manicured garden. The carriage stood waiting for her in front of the house, just where she left it.

Her eyes were dry by then, and her cheeks cooled. David, the coachman, sat up straighter at her approach before hopping down from his seat to open the carriage door. Judith had the presence of mind to favour him with a sideways smile and a wink entirely too warm to be given by a respectable woman to one of her household's servants. The young man coloured and shut the door behind her, before climbing back into place to take up the reins again. She smirked.

Entirely too useful, that one.

Her maid, Lucy, who she'd insisted wait for her in the carriage while she'd taken care of the whole business with the young Mrs Ellery, was leaning against the far interior wall, eyes closed, lips parted ungracefully. Judith decided to let her sleep, preferring quiet for the ride home.

As the wheels jounced her over the surface of the road, she rotated the small emerald ring she always wore on the middle finger of her right hand in that way she always did when her thoughts blotted out all else.

Her sister was far too innocent to be paddling around in the waters of intrigue. Not if she thought she'd be able to hide her splashings from Judith. When Graves had stormed out of the dining room after dessert that evening, it was completely obvious where Elinor was headed when she excused herself only moments later. Obvious to Judith, at least.

She hadn't found them in time to catch the pair in the act again, but after a methodical opening of door after door, she'd discovered everything she needed to know in the darkened guest room at the South end of the hall. The scent on the close air in the room alone was enough to make clear what had to have taken place within its walls.

So, she'd thought, as she'd fingered the rumpled linens at the edge of the bed that night, *an engagement to another man isn't enough incentive for you to leave off, is it Rowland Graves?*

If she couldn't put a stop to this whole ghastly affair by making her sister unavailable to him, then the next step was only rational. And the young Margaret Ellery would help her take it.

The rhythmic clattering of hooves ceased and the carriage came to a halt. Judith nudged the sleeping maid with the toe of her slipper.

"Wake up, Lucy."

"Mmm? Mrs Barlow?" The groggy woman blinked into the light coming in from the carriage window and stifled a yawn.

"We're home," she pointed out, needlessly.

Yes, home. Time to wait now. And watch. Her plan would either work or it wouldn't. If it didn't, well ... Judith would simply have to arrive at a new plan.

Rowland stared from one sombre face to another, his hands hanging helpless at his sides. It was as if he'd taken a stage to deliver a prepared speech, only to find his audience speaking another language entirely. His baffled silence was making it worse.

"I don't understand," he said, with a disoriented shake of his head. "How have I not been approved? Did you not receive Doctor Ellery's letter of recommendation?"

The greying, eternally waterlogged-looking Doctor Hooper raised a woolly silver brow at him from his seat at the centre of the long table. "We did. We also received his letter rescinding his recommendation, two days ago. And I suspect you know the why of it."

"What? No, I *don't* know 'the why of it.' I have no idea whatsoever!"

The other four Fellows, two seated on either side of Hooper, glowered back at him, their faces painted in a variety of expressions, ranging from judgement to disgust.

Am I in the right meeting? They haven't confused me for someone else? This is the twentieth of October, isn't it? As scheduled?

"No"—Hooper's voice rolled with cynicism—"I'm sure you haven't the faintest. Either way, Oxford's school of medicine has no room for that sort of business. Enough reputations have been tainted already, wouldn't you agree, Doctor Graves?" The older man's smirk pushed Rowland past bafflement and into irritation.

"What in Heaven's name are you talking about?" He wanted to fling his hat onto the floor in frustration. This professorship was supposed to have been all but secured, today's meeting a mere formality. He and Elinor should have been making plans to marry and move here already, and this man was turning the entire matter completely on its ear.

"Oh what indeed, Graves!" The man slapped his palm on the table. "You should know better than anyone what notorious gossips women are. Did you think your various episodes of impropriety would simply be kept quiet for your own convenience? That the daughters of gentlemen would stand for you running amok, taking advantage of their trust for your own gratification?"

Impropriety? Daughters? Plural?

"We won't stand for that sort of thing here," Hooper went on. "Do you know Doctor Ellery's letter tells us that one of the young women was engaged to be married? For shame, Sir! We've no interest in tainting our halls with scandals of that nature." He looked Rowland up and down as though eyeing something particularly unsavoury a dog had dragged into his house.

Engaged to be married?

There was exactly one person who could be behind this, though he still didn't understand why.

Judith Barlow.

Desperation flooded his veins, pouring out of his mouth.

"Doctor Hooper, there's been a mistake!" He stepped forward in his effort to explain. "Doctor Ellery has clearly been misinformed. If you'll simply allow me to—"

"To what, Graves? Poison our ears with more lies? I've known Francis Ellery for over forty years. I trust him with my very life, and you ask me not to believe his word?"

Hooper's accusations hung there, a black storm gathering over Rowland's head. His chest rose and fell in the condensed silence, the morning light partially silhouetting the table of Fellows, illuminating the condemning bald pates, but providing no warmth. His jaw shifted, tightly held, along with his gut.

"Perhaps you should consider a different line of work, *Doctor* Graves." Hooper filled the space in the room with his final pronunciation. "I don't think you've any future in medicine. At least not here."

And with those words, a door was closed.

So. It would be this way, would it?

Rowland narrowed his eyes at the array of Fellows who faced him from behind their table. Men who wouldn't listen. Who had made a decision based on a letter, to which they would hear no rebuttal, and which would affect them for only the span of this meeting, but would follow him for the rest of his career.

He knew men such as these. It was done.

Done.

"Very well," he said, his voice low, seething. "By your leave, *Gentlemen*." He took off his hat in a mockery of the normal respectful gesture before turning on his heel and striding from the room, not waiting to hear a formal dismissal.

He didn't even see the halls or grounds of his beloved Oxford, so dark and encompassing were this thoughts at his leave-taking. It was a blessing in disguise that no other soul crossed his path along the way. His angel was back in Bristol and there was no one here to inspire temperance and mercy in him the way she always did. And the portions of Rowland Graves roiling about on the surface on this chill October morning were neither temperate nor merciful at all.

III

Paved With Good Intentions

Five days. He had five days to spend alone in a carriage with his thoughts, and this was proving to be extremely unhelpful.

That was how long it would take to travel back with empty hands to Bristol. What would he tell Elinor when he got there? By what possible means could she persuade her father to see Rowland as a suitable husband now?

The sound of the carriage wheels ground out his thoughts, refining them as grain against a millstone.

Medicine had been his life, his calling. To delve deep, to discover the root of an ailment and cut or flush it out, to shake his fist and laugh at the weaknesses of the flesh, the vagaries of Fate. These things drove Rowland on in his quest for knowledge. But more, he truly wished to teach. To help other men learn the ways they could snatch the reins away from Fortune. To be a part of educating others, so that they might heal, might cure. A soul recovered at his hand was a shining reward, but the idea that he could show others, and that his teachings might cause dozens of men, scores, to go into the world and do the same …

And now it was gone. Thanks to that contemptible Judith Barlow.

His coachman was shouting something to another driver passing in the opposite direction. Rowland wished he would be silent.

How could someone as lovely and perfect as Elinor have a sister so vile and pestilent? They'd been brought up in the same household. He and his brother Jonathan weren't so different. Though his brother was more interested in ships and commerce than medicine, they shared most of the same sensibilities.

The one thing Rowland was certain of, though, was that it was indeed the elder Barlow sister who was behind this catastrophe. She'd already made use of her wiles to manufacture a sudden, convenient engagement, just before he'd planned to announce his own intentions. It was clear she'd discovered his involvement with Elinor, and she didn't approve. But why?

He popped his knuckles one by one as he sat, fermenting in his own ire within the shell of his carriage. Out the window the shadowless light of an overcast afternoon made the entire landscape look as he felt. Colourless. Oppressed. Hopeless.

And angry now, as well. A slow simmer of wrath, the sort normally doused by Elinor's patient, calming presence, was bubbling away inside him.

He reached into his coat pocket and brought out the scalpel. A gift, almost a jest, from Doctor Ellery, given upon his having earned his doctoral degree. Rowland never used it for actual practice; it was more of a sentimental token. Now, though, he applied it to removing non-existent dirt from under his already immaculate nails.

Who, exactly, did that shrew imagine she was toying with? First to meddle in his plans for engagement, and now to ruin his career? Daughters of gentlemen indeed! He suspected she knew very well her younger sister was far from unwilling, but to spread a tale of Rowland forcing himself? On both of them? He could see the lies dripping from her tongue, poisoning the goodwill of Francis Ellery. The man had been his mentor and now he would take Rowland for a knave, a defiler of young women. The interior of the carriage felt as if it was growing impossibly hot, despite the grey afternoon.

With a thump and a dull clatter, the carriage jolted over what must have been a sizable rock in the road. He heard the coachman give a low grunt outside, likely at being jostled in his seat.

A thin sting made Rowland look down to see a tiny, precise cut spelled out in red alongside the nail of his first finger. He glanced at the scalpel in his other hand before returning a blank stare to the cut. The thin scarlet line was welling up, becoming bloated under his gaze. His attention was rapt as it swelled into a precarious, wobbling ruby bead, swaying impossibly under the motion of the carriage before the tension broke at last and it escaped in a red path down the side of his finger.

He popped the digit into his mouth without thought. Blood didn't disturb him. How could it? Who could make a career as a medical man and have trouble with the sight? If he were honest with himself, he found it beautiful, in its own wet, macabre fashion. It was the most vibrant colour a body could make.

The most vibrant perhaps, but not the loveliest. Not by far. That honour he'd save for the pale delicate blue of Elinor's eyes. Or perhaps the white gold of her hair. The pink of her lips, or of her ...

Rowland returned the scalpel to his pocket, lest he cut something on purpose.

His angel was engaged to another man and now his future lay in ruins! How could this happen? How in two weeks could his universe be so upended?

You know precisely how, Rowland: the vicious meddling of a disapproving sister.

He squeezed at the tip of his finger and watched as another fat, ruddy pearl grew out of the cut. This time he held his hand upright and looked on as the droplet rolled down over his knuckle before losing volume and momentum in the valley between his first two fingers.

Other than the dull thud of hooves and the muted rolling of carriage wheels, it was so very quiet within the curved walls of the coach. Odd, he thought, as blood so often came with such a great deal of noise. Crying. Screaming. Pleading.

Rowland thought of such sounds. And he thought of Judith Barlow, destroyer of dreams. A doctor was supposed to make the pain stop, not awaken it. Not cultivate it like a fine, rare botanical specimen.

The bloodied hand had become a fist, and now his nails were dirty in truth, with red seeping beneath their edges.

Five days was too long to spend alone. He needed Elinor, needed her *now*. He never had these sort of thoughts if she was with him. His dove, his perfect angel, would chase this part of him away. Black, skittering things clawed at him, and her pure light could not come soon enough.

The light of early evening was bright enough, though low clouds covered the sky, but inside the carriage trundling westward towards Bristol, it was dark as a winter midnight.

Moonlight sliced the darkness inside the carriage house like a blade as the servants' door cracked open. He could see her from his place in the shadows, but she couldn't see him.

A step, and then another. She was coming closer.

Rowland caught her up, pulling her fast against him, silencing her startled gasp with a hand over her lips from behind.

"Does anyone know you're here?" he asked, as quietly as he was able. His fingers came away from her face, and he released her from his hold.

"No, my love," she whispered, straightening her shawl, eyes wide as they tried to adjust to the dark.

Praying for forgiveness, Rowland seized her up again in his embrace and captured her mouth in a hungry, desperate kiss. He couldn't stand to be in her presence and not touch her, not after the days of torture he'd spent alone on the road. As always, his angel knew without words what he needed and offered back yielding lips, a caressing tongue, and the faintest of approving whimpers.

"Rowland," she said in hushed tones when they finally parted, "we don't need to meet at midnight in my father's carriage house simply to trade kisses. What has happened?"

He set his forehead to hers, gripping her by the upper arms, unsure of how to explain, to tell what must be told. Delays would not improve matters, however.

"Oxford"—he managed to grind out—"did not go well, Dove. No, not well at *all*."

She held her tongue, waiting for him to continue.

"I won't be getting the professorship."

"But Rowland, that's terrible!" Her voice rose a bit louder than it ought to in her concern. "Why ever not?"

"Shhh, Love. It seems that ... it seems that Doctor Ellery has rescinded his recommendation. The Fellows will not approve me for the post."

Her palms came up to his chest, stroking in soothing lines over the front of his shirt. "I don't understand, Love," she said, "Doctor Ellery chose you himself to follow in his place. He introduced you to Father before he retired. Why would he—"

"Someone has filled his head with lies, Elinor. Someone has convinced him that I've behaved improperly with several 'daughters of gentlemen', including one already affianced."

The fine layer of grit on the floor crunched under the soles of his shoes as he shifted his stance, waiting for her to understand. He made an effort to loosen his grip on her arms. His angel was no place to leave the marks of his anger.

"Who would tell him such a thing?" Her tone was wound tight with confusion. It would do him good to remember that a soul as innocent as Elinor Barlow would not immediately see the root of trickery, even when it tripped her up at her feet.

"A person who doesn't want us to be together, Dove. A person who wants to make sure your father will *never* approve of me as a husband, who needs to see my future ruined to do so."

"But ... but ..." She was stepping away from him now, realisation washing over her. "How *could* she?"

"I don't understand it myself," he said, moving towards her again. "Why this hatred? What have I done to make an enemy of her? Family not agreeing on a suitor for a young lady, this I've heard of. But these lies? This sneaking and treachery in the dark? What sort of person does these things?"

The light was dim to the point of playing tricks on his eyes, but Rowland was sure he could see her shoulders begin to quake. A sniffle then, and a cough. He stepped forward in a rush, folding her into his arms, letting her hot cheek bury into the side of his neck.

"I'm sorry, Love. Please. Shhhh ..." He stroked at her hair, her back. "I didn't want to tell you. I'm sorry."

"She isn't my sister, Rowland," she said against his collar bone, almost too quietly to be heard.

"Oh, Love ..."

"No!" He felt her fingers tightening on his coat sleeves. "There's no reason! No reason at all for a person to be so wicked!"

Elinor's skin was flushed, heated against him wherever they touched, and he knew, in her own way, she was brushing against a bit of the same fury he'd known on his endless carriage ride. A nobler man would have been terribly distraught by the idea of his only love feeling this way, but certain grim, outlying facets of himself were beginning to make Rowland believe he might not be such a noble man.

If she hates her own sister, this will all be so much easier now, won't it?

He pushed the thought down. They were out here in this carriage house to discuss plans. Best to be about it.

"Elinor."

Hearing her name seemed to break her from her spiral of despair and she tilted her face up to him.

"Do you want us to be together?"

"You know I do!"

"It seems hope is lost for us here in Bristol," he began, chest tightening in anticipation of how she might react. "Will you come away with me?"

"To where, my love?"

A fine start. She had not balked or rejected the idea out of hand. He ploughed ahead.

"Amsterdam. My cousin Ruth married a printer some three years ago, and her husband set up his business there. I'm sure they would take us under their roof for a time, at least until I could establish myself."

"But ... Amsterdam?" She sounded sceptical. "Will your cousin not simply relay your whereabouts to your family? And if Judith suspects ... will my family not come asking yours about where you've disappeared to?"

"She hasn't spoken to my father's side of the family since her wedding. I don't think they much approved of her choice of husband, either. I'm sure she'll keep her silence, if I ask it."

His angel was still with indecision in his arms. He could nearly feel the churn of her considering.

"Elinor?"

Silence.

"Yes. We'll do it. We'll go to Amsterdam."

He might have broken her in half, he squeezed her to him so tightly then.

"Thank you, my love! Thank you!" He all but twirled her about. "Now we must only think of a way to—"

"I have a way."

"You do?" He held her now at arm's length, blinking into the darkness. It was his turn to be caught off guard.

"Yes. The feast. Do you remember? At the end of the month? The one Father has planned on Hallowtide?"

"The one you insisted I had that silly raven mask made for? With the odd name? Where did he get the idea for that again?" He took up her hand and pulled her deeper into the darkened building, peering about for somewhere they could sit.

"The *masquerade*. Yes. And it was Mr Ashford's idea, one of Father's friends. He spent the last year in Venice; it seems this sort of thing is the latest style there." Rowland had spied out a low bench against the rear wall and sat, drawing her onto his knee. "If you ask me," she said, giggling quietly against his ear, "Mr Ashford must have shown Father the bottom of *several* glasses of wine, Love. He'd normally never agree to an event such as this. At least not after Mother died."

As much as it relieved him to hear her calming from her earlier upset, Rowland didn't understand how this odd party was going to help them, and he said as much.

"Don't you see, Rowland?" She straightened, doing her best to look him in the eye in the dark. "It's perfect. There will be so many faces hidden behind masks, no one will know who's going where or top from bottom. You can find me there and we'll slip away before anyone is the wiser."

His heart swelled with pride at such clever words from his angel. Framing her lovely face with both his hands, he kissed her again, wanting to consume her with approval.

"Brilliant," he said. "You surprise me every day, Elinor."

She wriggled on his knee at his words and threw her arms about his neck, and for a time they fell to dappling each other in sweet, hopeful kisses.

"How will I know you?" he asked once they settled.

"You'll see me in black with the face of a raven, but how will I find you?"

"I'll be in grey and white," she said, leaning her head against his shoulder. "I had a mask made to look like a dove. Since that's what you always call me." He could almost feel her blushing in the dark, and he stroked at the back of her hand with his fingertips.

Something in him began to coil about, however, the first burn of venom lapping at his insides. His throat tightened.

"That sister of yours will be there ... won't she."

It was not a question.

"Yes, Rowland." He could tell by Elinor's voice she'd rather he'd not brought it up. He found himself unable to resist another jab.

"And what will *she* be dressed as? A serpent?"

The Devil himself?

"You're horrible!" She aimed a half-hearted swat at him, though he suspected the vehemence of her protest was dulled considering her current disposition towards her elder sister. "She'll be in russet and black. She chose to have a mask fashioned after a fox."

Rowland *harrumphed* to himself. A fox. Almost as appropriate as his guess of 'serpent.' His mind was not truly on costumes, though.

"I think I may know how we can find our way to Amsterdam," he told her. "Once your father finds you missing, Bristol Port will be watched. My brother is assistant to the Harbourmaster, you know—he'll be the first one your family will seek out once they realise what's happened."

"Then what will we do?" she asked, her voice offering complete faith that he would have an answer as she tangled her slim fingers up in the dark queue of his hair where it trailed down his neck.

"I'll have a carriage waiting. I'll find you at this ... *masquerade* ... and tell you where to meet me. We'll leave for London and sail from there instead, where no one will be looking for us. I've enough money saved, I'm sure of it. I'll take everything, to be safe."

"Oh, Rowland! Will we truly do this? I want to be yours but ... my family? Yours? Will we ever see them again?"

"I don't know, Love," he said, truthful though it pained him to be. Rowland gathered her against him, burying his face in the smooth skin under her jaw, hiding from the possibility she might change her mind.

He could feel her pulse against his lips, and he let its warm rhythm calm him as he waiting for her next words in the silence.

"We'll go," she said at last. "It's the only way. I love you, Rowland."

"And I love you."

Yes. The only way.

His mind whirled with ravens and doves as he held her. Ships and carriages, and his eyes clenched tight in the darkness. Foxes and single drops of blood on the road between here and Oxford. Nothing further would be allowed to hinder them.

The only way.

✧

The Hatchet Inn was noisy, but it suited him well enough. Graves wanted to be away from his family this night, from any of his normal circles for that matter, and so, as he often did when his affairs were troubling him, he called upon Bernard Helsby.

"It's only three days, Graves. You've only to stay with your first plan, which is mad enough, if I do say. There's no need for all the rest."

Helsby frowned into his mug, avoiding Rowland's eye as he prodded his friend towards reason.

"Isn't there?" Rowland's voice was tired as he leaned back against the wall of the common room, sloshing his own drink in lazy circles.

He eyed the man sitting next to him, sturdily built and, as his clothing indicated, not of the same social sphere as Rowland at all. Helsby's father had been farrier to Rowland's family, among others, for ages, and the two had been boys together. Though one had followed in his father's trade and the other had gone on to Oxford, they always seemed to know how to find each other when an ear was needed on either side.

"You'll have the girl!" the other man said, looking up at last. "This other bit? Revenge? It's pointless! Just sail for Amsterdam and have done."

"It isn't revenge, Friend," he tried to explain, setting his own mostly empty mug back on the table, "It's only a preventative measure. She's maliciously fouled my plans twice now. Who's to say she won't find some way to do it again? And we'll be in Amsterdam before my Elinor is any the wiser."

"Do you hear yourself, Graves?" Helsby hissed at him, darting a quick glance about the room. "This isn't some business matter, old friend. What you speak of is … well, it's *murder*!" He huffed out the last word in a low breath, and now Rowland, too, cast an eye about. A man shifted position at the end of the long table, but he appeared to be somewhere near sleep with his head in the crook of an arm. Hearing a faint snort from the drunk, Rowland turned his attention back to the one person he trusted aside from Elinor.

He sighed, pushing his fingers through his hair. "I know. I know what it is, Helsby."

"Then don't do it!" the other, more sober man snapped at him under his breath. Rowland turned his head to the side and blinked at his friend. The room swam a bit and he decided this would need to be his last drink for the night.

Reassure him, Rowland. It was a mistake to think you could confess such an idea, even to him.

The merest hint of a laugh heaved out of him and he

graced his confidante with a wry look. "You know I won't, Helsby. Can you imagine such a thing? I'm merely furious and full of ale."

The other man shook his head and mopped at his brow with the back of a sleeve, downing another draught as though his friend had put him in need of it. "You're full of something, *Doctor* Graves, I'll warrant you that. Just you dress up as a … as a … crow was it?"

"A raven."

"Yes, a raven, and steal away with this dove of yours and be a happy man far away from Bristol. And get some sleep, for pity's sake. You look wretched."

"You're right, Helsby. You're always right. Especially about the sleep."

The two men finished their mugs and talk turned to other subjects, but Rowland felt the sour taste of guilt on the back of his tongue. He'd let his friend believe it was the drink talking and that he was not serious at all about his intentions for the elder Barlow sister.

It was unfortunate for nearly everyone involved that this was not the case. His mind had been humming all evening with frightful schemes and, to his increasing dread, even thoughts of his angel, Elinor, could not banish them. An end to the cause, he thought, could surely be an end to the symptom as well. And if there was one thing Rowland Graves knew how to do, it was to find a cure for that which ailed.

✦

The scullery was a distasteful place for a woman of her status to be skulking about at this hour of the night, but it was the first room accessible from the servants' entrance and so was the easiest place for her to meet the coachman. At least it was if she wanted to keep their meeting secret, and she most surely did that.

"Did you follow like I asked?" she said, taking a step

backwards to lean against the door to the yard, pulling the young man after her by the lapels of his livery coat so he stood in unseemly proximity. His throat moved as he swallowed in the candlelight.

Such a beast, to be led around by the nose this way.

"I did, Mrs Barlow." He didn't back away from her, though. Judith knew he'd be tempted by her offer of more than what was proper.

"And did you learn anything useful, David?" Not only did she call him by his given name, but she arched against him now, and watched as the subtle move caused him to struggle with keeping his hands to himself.

Generous with the trowel this evening, are we, Judith?

"It seems ..." He leaned in, and she allowed him to rest a hand at her waist.

A small price to pay.

She kept the inviting smirk on her lips.

"What does it seem?" she said, voice barely a breath, tilting her head just to one side, exposing the length of her throat. He took the bait and bent his face to her neck, inhaling all that he was infatuated with, all that was above his station.

"It seems he intends to flee Bristol with your sister."

It was not news a body wanted to hear when some man, a servant, was brushing his lips under one's jawline. Judith curled her lip in disgust, though the coachman didn't see it.

Somehow, it hadn't come as a surprise. Rowland Graves was a determined man. Perhaps not so much as Judith Barlow, he might soon discover. There was no possible way she could allow him to leave with Elinor.

She schooled herself into an appropriate veneer of feminine surrender as the male body she'd tempted pressed more fully against her. The hand that had been at her waist had now found its way into her hair. The coachman would do anything she asked, as long as he continued to believe he had a chance.

The things I put up with! Is he ... is he hard? Heaven, give me patience.

"Is that all, David?" Her voice was still a honeyed purr, betraying none of her inner irritation.

"No." His lips had moved to the top of her shoulder, and she shrugged, nudging his mouth away so he would finish his thought. The knave was bold now, and undeterred, but he spoke all the same between kisses at her collar bone. "I think ... he may be planning ... to kill you."

There it was. Judith didn't care what the coachman kissed now. She knew this had been coming, as well, and the last of her suspicions were forming together.

Once or twice she'd seen it. Doctor Rowland Graves had that singular, subtle dark flash in his eye. The sort that, if a person knew what they were seeing, spoke of a man who was capable of unspeakable things. Likely no one would have noticed it aside from Judith. She knew the look all too well. It stared back at her each day in the mirror.

She sighed. It was about time to push the eager David away from her again. His hands were becoming a bit too free.

Her sister wasn't meant for Rowland Graves, a fact the man hardly seemed to realise. Perhaps it was time for Judith to stop being ... subtle.

✦

"What do you want, Judith?"

"To speak with you, Sister."

"If you must," Elinor said, a cold, stubborn tilt to her jaw as she sat still for the busy hands and heated tongs of her maid. The servant buzzed about, curling and piling up golden hair on top of her head in preparation for the evening's festivities.

"Might it be in private?" she asked, eyeing the hovering maidservant.

Her younger sister narrowed her eyes in the mirror and

gave an irritated sigh so pointed, it nearly ended in a growl.

"Very well," she said, and turned to the maid who had stepped back, curling tongs still in hand. "Hope, will you please leave us?"

The girl graced her mistress with a nod and scuttled out of the room. Her quick steps said she was eager to remove herself when lightning all but crackled in the air between both sisters the way it did now.

When the door closed behind her, Elinor turned on the low stool where she sat to face Judith, arching a brow in her direction.

And we begin.

"I know about you and Doctor Graves," Judith said.

To her credit, Elinor actually sneered at her. Sneered! It seemed her sister might be growing a backbone after all these years.

"Of course you do!" Elinor said. "Do you imagine me blind? I know you spoke to Father. I know it was you behind those awful rumours that cost Doctor Graves his professorship. And now I'm stuck in this ridiculous engagement, and his career is lost! Just what do you believe you're playing at?" She appraised Judith from top to bottom as she said these words, as if she weren't sure who she was addressing.

"Sister, I—"

"Don't call me that! You are *not* my sister!"

Judith ground her teeth. This was to be expected. She pushed on.

"I am only looking out for your well-being," she said, taking a supplicating step towards the angry, quivering woman sitting before her. "Doctor Graves is ... well, he's ... he's taking advantage of you! Don't you see? The things he's convinced you to do? Unwed? The man is a scoundrel, Elinor. You're far too good for him."

"A scoundrel!" her sister cried, gripping fistfuls of her dressing gown in her dainty hands, pale blue eyes blazing.

"How dare you! After all the lies you've told! The deceptions! Perhaps you should place such names on yourself!"

"I was trying to protect you!"

Soon. We're very close now to the break.

"Protect me from what? Love?" Elinor stood up, knocking the stool over in her fury. "I *love* him! Simply because *you* haven't found love doesn't mean *I* should be kept from it!"

Her sister had stepped close into Judith's space, her face red and eyes flashing. The elder Barlow sister made her features impassive and said nothing.

Wait for it ...

"You must ..." Elinor began again, her voice quavering this time, "You must *hate* me to have done these things! Well it won't matter, Judith. Tonight is the last you'll be forced to see the one you loathe so much. I'm leaving! *We're* leaving. Doctor Graves will find me at the *masquerade* and we'll be gone! We'll marry elsewhere and you won't have to look at either of us ever again!"

There we go. Take hold of the wheel, Judith. It's time to steer this ship ...

The impassioned speech had left her younger sister's face striped with hot tears and her voice broken. Judith took a step back, and lowered her tone to that of quiet shock.

"You ... you love him?"

"Of *course* I do!"

The abrupt change in the conversation's flavour was too much for Elinor, and she collapsed onto the rug under buckling knees and a stream of new tears. "Of course I do, you fool," she repeated, sobbing quietly, her gaze on the floor now.

Judith sank to the carpet with her.

"Elinor, I didn't *know*," she said, voice quieted now, taking up her sister's limp hand. "I thought ... well ... you're only twenty-two, and he's two years older than *I* am. I simply thought he was trying to get what *all* men want, and acting the knave with you. I didn't want you to be hurt."

The sound of her pleading sincerity was impressive, she thought, though there was no time for self-congratulation just yet. Her sister sniffled and met her eyes, red-rimmed blue to deep brown in the afternoon light. Judith pressed on.

"Sister, I'm sorry. I truly wanted what was best. For you to be happy."

It seemed Elinor's expression softened for a moment, before she wiped at an eye with the back of her hand.

"I'm still leaving, you know," she said, sniffling, eyes on their joined hands. "Father will never allow me to marry him now."

Judith let out a weak laugh. "I know. I know you are."

"This will be goodbye, then," her sister said, looking back up at her.

Now.

"Elinor, why would you think Father would let you leave the *masquerade*? He'll have his eyes on you all night. An engaged young woman? Unchaperoned? You won't make it out of his sight. He was there when the seamstress delivered the gowns—he knows to keep an eye on the dove for the evening."

"But I *must* leave tonight!" Elinor tightened her grip, a pleasing note of desperation in her voice. "Doctor Graves has it all arranged! He'll have a carriage waiting. I don't think there will be another chance!"

Judith shifted her weight. Sitting this way on the floor was growing uncomfortable.

Give it to her. Give her hope.

"Sister," she said, as if a thought had just occurred to her, "Father will be watching a *dove* all night."

Elinor blinked at her, uncomprehending.

"He won't be paying nearly as much attention to a fox."

Blue eyes grew round.

"Judith …" she said, in a tone of both wonder and accusation.

"Yes! People mistake us for one another all the time if they haven't seen our faces! Do you remember when Henry tried to give you a fright on Christmas Eve, but it was me he started and I nearly fell down the stairs? And then you came up from behind him just then and he *did* fall? You'd think he saw a ghost!"

Elinor was giggling now at the memory of their witless cousin and his attempt at a jest. This was good.

"Elinor if you wear my gown and fox mask, and I dress the part of the dove, Father will have his eyes on me and not you. You'll be able to slip away, I'm sure of it!"

She watched her excitement spread to her sister, but it faded back into a frown in a heartbeat.

"But if I'm wearing *your* gown, how will Doctor Graves find me? I told him I'd be dressed in grey, as a dove."

Judith put all the warmth she had into her smile. "Why Sister, that's no trouble at all. When he approaches me as the dove he believes to be you, I'll simply tell him we've exchanged gowns and point you out to him."

The way Elinor gaped at this solution was priceless. There was a long moment of staring before she drew her hand back.

"Why?" Suspicion rolled back over her features. "Why would you do this thing for me?"

And now for the last course: dessert.

"Because I, too, have found love."

The shock could not have been more complete.

"You love someone?" Elinor said. "Who?"

"Someone I can never be with, Sister." It was Judith's turn to look at the floor. "Someone Father would never let me have, either."

"Who?"

"I won't say his name. A servant."

"One of *our* servants?" Elinor squeaked, snatching up the thread of gossip.

"Sister, *please*," she said, fending her off. "There is nothing to be done about it. You asked why I will help you now? This is why. One of us, at least, should be with her Love."

Eyes welling up again, Elinor threw her arms about Judith, all but suffocating her in an embrace.

"I didn't *want* to hate you, Sister!" She sobbed into the familiar shoulder. "Please forgive me! I'm sorry!"

"I'm sorry, too." Judith returned the embrace, staring up at the pattern of the drapes as she received forgiveness she hadn't earned. "I'm sorry I have to lose you to make it right."

The Barlow sisters came together again as they knelt on the bedroom carpet, each filled with a very different set of hopes, come the end of Hallowtide.

✧

IV

The Dove and the Fox

✧

There she was. The fox. Though not such a clever beast as Rowland Graves, she would find.

He'd been watching Judith make her way around the crowded room all evening, with occasional discreet glances for his angel, as well.

Elinor was lovely in grey and the smiles he caught from under her dove mask whenever their eyes met across the room were enough to reassure him of the worth of what he meant to do.

It was only a matter of time. There would be so many glasses of wine and no more before a lady—loosely as that term might be applied to the harpy who wore the fox mask—would need to excuse herself.

Rowland contributed a false laugh to the conversation he was feigning an interest in, and sipped a bit more from his own glass, waiting. Watching.

Ah. There.

The elder Barlow sister was making her way towards one of the doors that lead to the hallway.

He excused himself.

There were but two directions a person could go, he noted, as he stepped into the corridor himself, and one of them led to the kitchens. She would not be going that way. Rowland turned the other way and stole along.

Near the foot of the stairs there was an alcove, and he ducked into it, making himself still against the wall. His black garb and the darkened hallway would hide him from notice. All he need do was wait: there was only one way back into the *masquerade*.

Rowland's heart pounded as he held himself there, eyes on the top step, at the landing. There would be no going back once he did this. Once he set this plan into motion tonight, there would be no choice but to see it through to its sordid, shameful end.

Elinor must never find out. She may say she hates her sister, but she will never forgive you this. She cannot know you're capable of such a horror.

A figure turned the corner above him and began its descent. As the feminine form drew near, he saw the russet and black silks, the fox mask. She had come to the bottom step, and was looking away from the place he hid.

Now! Do it now!

With a smooth, silent step he was behind her, his right arm coming around her throat. He clamped down on her neck at once from either side with his upper arm and forearm, right hand gripping his left shoulder, squeezing, preventing her from drawing another deceitful breath.

She clawed at him and her heels dug at the carpet, small strangled sounds thrumming against his constricting arm. His left hand however, had flown to the back of her head, fingers sliding into the mountain of curls, forcing her neck to bend forward.

Her noises were muted by the compression on her frantic, flexing throat, and he held her fast. It would only take a moment, and …

Hands dropped away from his arms, the body softened, and then went limp. He would need to be quick now.

Glancing about again to be sure the hall was still empty of prying eyes, he stepped back into the alcove, hauling his temporary rag doll with him. Rowland lowered her to the floor and leaned her against the side of the alcove in a sitting position, though in her current state her head lolled forward.

In a flurry of silent, deft movements he did what was needful. A wadded handkerchief served to stuff into her slack mouth and he secured in place with a soft leather strap as a gag for when she inevitably woke. Strips of a bed sheet he'd cut up that morning bound her wrists and ankles within the tense space of a few breaths.

His parcel secure, Rowland surveyed the hall a final time. Not a soul in sight. He knelt and hoisted the bundle over his shoulder, the dead weight twice as heavy now, and wasted no time hurrying on with his mad scheme.

Now he *would* go towards the kitchen, his strides speeding him along, but instead of turning left, into a room he knew would be crowded with busy servants, he kept straight on. At the very end of the hallway there was another door. He balanced the limp body of Judith Barlow on his shoulder and fumbled for the latch.

Cool night air washed over his grim face. He stepped outside and closed the door. Hell would be worth it, he kept telling himself, if it meant nothing would stand between him and his angel, at least while he still walked the earth.

✦

She was awake. Squirming. Weeping it seemed. It was a sound he was surprised she had the capacity to make. One rather expected curses out of a woman the likes of Judith Barlow. Muffled curses, at least.

He picked his way along the dark streets, preferring the shadows. The new moon was still a week away, but clouds obscured the luminous semi-circle this night. The bundle lashed behind his saddle gave the occasional jerk as it struggled against a fate it had brought on itself.

Rowland had first thrown a sack over her head, as soon as he'd made it from the Barlow house to his waiting horse. He didn't want to look at her. He'd then tucked a blanket around her bound form. He didn't want anyone else who might happen by looking, either.

It hadn't helped that she'd chosen the moment he was securing her bulk over the dappled rump of the mare to awaken and begin thrashing about. He was thankful the cloth and leather gag kept most of her frantic noises down to a fairly inconspicuous level. As his horse plodded on, threats of the scalpel ensured more satisfactory levels of quiet.

Hallowtide was an odd night in Bristol, and perhaps most places in England. It was decades since any Catholic wanted to admit their faith, at least not while standing in the shadow of the Church of England. Days like tomorrow and the next, All Saints' and All Souls', for those who confessed their sins and offered secret prayers to Mother Mary, did not see much public observance at all.

People, however, were creatures of habit, and did not like to give up old traditions. The streets, especially the narrow ones Rowland kept to, were deserted on this night. Be it custom or superstition, a man did not wander outside on Hallowtide after dark, lest he encounter a lost spirit. Yes, there were those superstitious folk—more of the population than would care to admit—who still believed the souls of the dead could walk the earth at this time of year.

It was nonsense, of course, but he was glad to take advantage of the empty streets and the cover of dark. If people were afraid, and it worked in his favour, so be it.

"You know, Mrs Barlow," he said in a low voice to the prone bundle behind him, "I would have even called your efforts clever, and been secretly impressed with them, had they not been taken out against me. Very neat, that business with Doctor Ellery. I looked a right fool in front of the Fellows."

The bundle let out a dull grunt of frustration. Rowland chuckled to himself. Their destination was almost upon them.

"Yes, I don't think I've ever truly known hatred until our recent crossing of paths." His voice was casual, almost matter-of-fact, but his grip on the reins made his knuckles ache. "Have you seen your sister cry because one of her own kin has betrayed her? I have. No one should be allowed to cause that amount of pain to such a sweet little dove."

Further dampened squealing and restrained bucking. The bindings were true, though, and struggle though she might, Judith Barlow would not be evading the preventative measures he intended for this night. Measures that would bar her from further interference in his and Elinor's happiness. For ever.

"Perhaps you've never known love," he mused, approaching the walls of the cemetery. "Perhaps that's why it was so easy to play at ripping it away from someone else. *I* know love, *Judith*. I love your sister. And neither you, nor any other force on this earth is going to stand in the way of it."

His words finished with a snarl as he brought the mare to a halt and dismounted. Desperate sobbing from the viper tied over the back of his horse.

"You'll earn no pity from me, woman," he said as he led the mare along on foot now, making his way towards his goal.

He nearly didn't see it at first, with the clouded night sky giving him almost no light, but a set of lines too straight, a shape too bright in the darkness, led him to what he sought. Rowland dropped the reins and the horse stayed as she ought.

Kneeling, he shoved the lid aside with as little noise as it was possible for him to make. The spade was within as promised, and the hastily built wooden coffin lay beside the agreed-upon ready hollow in the earth. A purse in the hands of a sexton, it seemed, would go a long way. When said hands had a fondness for lifting drink to lips, it went even further.

Quick now, Rowland. Do this thing and return to your angel.

The coffin had been heavy enough without the weight of a body in it, and so he'd chosen to lower it first and then go about filling it. It was no small task to manoeuvre the box down into the hole without making a horrible racket, and he found himself sweating despite the cool night air when he'd managed it. He shed his coat once he'd hoisted himself back out. It was time to fetch the fox.

There would be no telling what sort of mad pleas she was offering as he loosened the ties that bound her to the horse, but she was surely letting loose a string of them from behind the gag. He slid the body onto the damp earth and watched with something leagues beyond disdain as it wriggled about. With a grip under her arms, he pulled her towards the grave. The sack he left in place over her head; he still did not want to look at her. Perhaps if he couldn't see the face of a live person, the deed might be done with more ease.

His words, however, as he hauled her after him into the waiting cavity, appeared to come from a different place. A place long divorced from hesitation or humanity.

"Do you know where you are, Judith Barlow?" he whispered to her as he wrestled her bucking form into place between the six wooden walls. "Do you know what the inside of a coffin feels like?"

The thrashing and muffled screams at these words were like nothing he'd ever seen as he fitted the lid in place, and Rowland had seen quite the variety of people in pain. The intervening layer of wood further muted the noises, and they were now accompanied by a storm of dull thuds and thumps from frantic knees and shoulders within.

Don't think about it, Graves. Just have an end to it.

A second ascent from the earth brought him back to the spade, and the mindless work of filling the hollow began. His thoughts moved in to devil him as he shifted the dirt.

Perhaps he was a coward, for achieving his aims this way. The eventual weight of the earth, denying air to desperate lungs inside an enclosed space would do his horrific work for him, and he would not have to wring the life out with his bare hands. Either way, the body would be hid and the deed done.

The grave was still far from filled before he could no longer hear the feral noises coming from within the box. The silence bought him a measure of relief, and he tried to think of Elinor and Amsterdam as he put his back into the remainder of the work.

You and I, Love. You and I. Once I have you in my arms again, this terrible night will be a dream, I swear it. There's only good for us now. Only good.

The ground had flattened out sometime during his litany of silent promises to Elinor. Rowland laid the spade aside, mopping at his brow.

It was done.

He'd done the one thing he couldn't take back. The crime that would buy him peace with his angel.

He need only return to the *masquerade* and collect his little dove, and they could set out for their new life. If it wouldn't make so much noise, he would have set the mare to a run.

I'm coming, Elinor.

✦

Guests were stifling yawns and casting their eyes about in that distracted way that said they were looking for excuses to make their goodbyes and leave the *masquerade*. It appeared Rowland had returned with little time to spare.

Clear streets would be better for his and Elinor's leave-taking.

He found her across the room, engaged in what appeared to be polite conversation with a tall man wearing a mask made to look like a lion, or some other great cat, and a coat of gold brocade. The man gave his angel a small bow and wandered off, however, while Rowland made his way around the edge of the room towards her.

She stood alone when he brought himself near, though he kept his eyes elsewhere as though the raven and the dove were paying each other no attention whatsoever. When he found himself close enough, he spoke to her under his breath, gaze on a platter of sweet meats.

"The carriage is outside in the place I spoke of. We can't be seen leaving at the same time. Go first, and I will follow shortly. Wait for me inside the carriage."

His quiet instructions delivered, he meandered off, taking an ostensible interest in a laughing group of men on the far side of the room. Rowland knew she'd heard him by the way she'd sidled closer when he began to speak. No need to risk both of them speaking and doubling the possibility of discovery. Out of the corner of his eye, he now saw the grey and white shape of her gown floating towards one of the doors.

Perfect.

It was all he could do to hold back the urge to stride out on her heels and hustle her into the carriage himself. He wanted to be away from this house, now. Abraham Barlow was soon to become far less fond of Doctor Ellery's protégé, and he meant to be well away from Bristol by that time.

A full quarter of an hour he mingled with the other guests, answering dreadfully dull questions with false attentiveness, all the while gnawing at the inside of his cheek and clenching his gut tight with compressed urgency. When at last it seemed as though a reasonable amount of time had passed between her exit and his, he managed to make his excuses and show the room his back.

The night air was a welcome balm to his nearly fevered flesh as he made his way towards the waiting carriage. It was a chore to hold himself in check and not run.

His coachman made to come down from the seat to open the door when he saw Rowland approach, but with a brisk nod and a gesture, he stayed where he was and set the team of four into motion as soon as the man in the raven mask had stepped inside and closed the door.

With the curtains on the carriage windows drawn closed, there was precious little light inside the confines of the coach, but the pale mass opposite him could only be his dove. He slid into place beside her on the bench, relief cleansing away his tension and fear.

There was no reason to be discreet any longer. He gathered her up with greedy arms, drawing her onto his lap. A tiny sound of surprise broke on her lips, but he shushed her.

"Shh, Angel. It's just us now. Let us be silent, and not alert the driver."

The whispered suggestion seemed enough, as she settled into place at his words, resting her back against his chest in the still, dark space.

For a time, he did no more than clasp her to him, his arms a tight circle around her waist, woefully inconsiderate of how her stays must be already digging in. Rowland wasn't sure, though, if it was the sigh that undid him, or her laying her head back on his shoulder to bare some of her throat. It was no matter; his angel needed to do but the smallest thing to stir his blood.

Loosening the hold of his arms a bit, he lowered his face to her neck. A delicious heat purred like silk across his lips, as it always did. He set his mouth to her, gentle at first, but soon with a greater hunger. Her fingers covered one of his hands at her waist.

Heaven. I've bought a brief stay in Heaven this night by condemning my soul into Hell.

Her scent filled him up with each breath, a different perfume tonight, it seemed. Of course his angel would want something special for their first night of freedom together. A nip at her ear brought a restrained moan, and as he nuzzled the side of his face against hers he felt that she still wore her dove mask, as he did his raven. Something about this made him painfully hard, and he shifted his hips to bind himself less.

Soft caresses fell behind, abandoned for fervour in short order. One of his hands had wandered up to her breast, and he stroked a thumb over the rise of flesh above her neckline before dipping his hand beneath the edge of her gown. She hissed at this bold venture and he gathered up the warm globe in his palm, pulling its hardened tip between his fingers.

Her hand had found its way to the back of his neck and, to the further destruction of his self-control, her backside was rolling against the crook of his lap in a most wanton fashion.

You're a miracle, Elinor. I don't know if I deserve you.

It was clear what would happen, right here in this very carriage. Their need was simply too great.

The hand that had been at her breast was now tangled in skirts and petticoats, gathering material aside as his kisses trailed up the side of her raised arm. She was astonishingly wet when he found her with his fingertips, and he might as well have choked on his responding groan.

Here you are telling her *to be quiet!*

His lovely, surrendering dove brought her knees outside of his and tilted her hips for him. His fingers accepted the invitation. He teased and delved and slid, revelling in her responses as she writhed in his lap. It was both a magnificent and excruciating idea to shush her occasional whimpers by sliding the first two fingers of his other hand into her mouth. She began suckling at him at once and he nearly unravelled.

Rowland Graves was reckless in his lust. Their compulsion to silence magnified the feverish sound of their breath hurrying in and out, and brought his attention to every jerk of her hips and rise of her breast. He slid the wet fingers from her mouth down to capture a tight nipple again and toy with it, while his other hand busied itself in making his little dove squirm with delight.

The clenching of her flesh around his fingers proved to be too much. Pulling his hands away from her body, he began piling up masses of fabric in a fury. She sensed what he was about at once and raised her bottom away from him, pulling the rest of the material out of the way herself.

He had breeches fumbled aside in the space of a breath. Elinor lowered herself so his hot length rode up against the soaking furrow between her thighs. He moved his hips to glide along the wet heat, and to his utter delight, she reached down with dainty fingers to grasp and stroke him, her hand slick with her own moisture.

Always ask permission, Rowland.

He remembered his promise to himself through a haze of desire, and felt the need to keep it, though he wanted to be quiet. A word would have to suffice.

"Please," he breathed, hoping his question was clear.

When she angled him and sank her full weight down on his straining cock, he took that for assent. She was exquisite, as always.

Hands at her hips now, he wasted no time falling into the cycle of plumb and draw he needed so very much. He felt full and heavy inside her clutching walls. Soft, rolling, tongues of flame were licking low in his belly, and he began to drive up into her with a desperate will.

As he pushed and worked, bent on release, his right hand found hers at her side and he laced their fingers together. His thrusts became more erratic as he approached the edge, and her grip tightened on his hand, pinching some ring she was wearing painfully between their fingers.

Odd, I don't remember her ever wearing any rings.

In the midst of his building climax he felt a set of dainty fingertips tracing over the skin of his bouncing scrotum, and colours flashed behind his eyelids. He drove into her now with astonishing violence and sank his teeth into the curve between her neck and shoulder. This beastly turn became too much for his angel, and she gasped and choked out his name.

"Rowland!"

Paralysis.

It was not Elinor's voice

It was *not* Elinor's voice!

Horror. A flash. A sundering of bodies. He couldn't breathe.

The blunt, abrupt impact against the wall of his back might have come from either the carriage door as he tumbled backwards out of it, or the accusing blow of the earth when he met it as he skittered away from the implosion of wrongness inside the still-moving coach.

Either way, that one call of his name had unmade his world, and Rowland Graves scrambled to his feet and fled from reality on shaking legs into the night.

✦

"Rowland! Wait!"

The black, fluttering shriek of her voice darted after him, pricking his skin as he ran stumbling over damp grass and earth, headlong into his nightmare. His mind was a void of denial as he flew, but jagged fissures of terror threatened to breach the abyss.

Impossible.

Run! There is nothing! Run!
Impossible!

Something yanked at the flapping hem of his coat. A pulling weight made him spin about and one of his shoes slid in the loose dirt. Hands out, he braced for the inevitable fall, only to find himself landing in a tangled mass of limbs and petticoats. A voice on the verge of tears burst out of the woman he now straddled.

"Please!"

His arms shook, uninterested in supporting his weight over the fallen body beneath him. There was a buzzing between his ears and, for a brief time, as he struggled with the task of breathing, not a single coherent thought formed in Rowland's mind.

When at last the notions came, they came one at a time, as if he had no means to process more than one at once.

Judith Barlow.

He wrenched the dove mask away from her face, drawing a pained squeal from her as its ties snapped. The night was dark, but so were the eyes he could barely see. Elinor's were pale blue.

Elinor was the dove. Judith was the fox. Trap the fox, free the dove. That was the plan.

His weight was on her shoulders as well now as he pinned her with his palms, chest heaving.

"What have you done?"

The voice that came out of him was almost inhuman.

"Please, Rowland!"

A crisp slap cut off her wailing plea as his palm made a sharp connection with her cheekbone before returning to her shoulder.

"What have you *DONE*?"

"It was the only way!" She burst out sobbing. "I had to! Rowland, listen to me! I—"

Another, sharper slap, and he slammed her shoulders against the ground for good measure.

"How *dare* you call me by my Christian name! And what do you mean 'the only way'? The only way for *what*?" He was unhinged now. Rabid.

"For us to be together!"

Even Chaos stopped its spinning. Rowland's breath hitched and he blinked down at her in the gloom. All was still.

"I tried to show you, my love, but—"

"*Never* call me that!" he roared, his fingers digging into the flesh of her shoulders like claws. She seemed not to notice, though, and her mad words tumbled on in a rush.

"But you wouldn't see! She was too good for you! Too innocent! My sister could *never* be what you need! But you were both so blind! She wouldn't be convinced, and neither would you! You could have just seen reason with her engagement to Dunning, but you wouldn't! I had to make her unavailable to you! So you would see!"

Her speech was a torrent of insanity and he lowered his face to within inches of hers, snarling, surges of dead light beginning to come in at the edges of his vision.

"So I would see *what*? *Judith*?" He spat her name like a curse.

The look of utter, senseless devotion he saw in the lines of her face then made him want to be ill. The viper went limp and pliant beneath him.

"I know what you are, Rowland," she said, as if the words were a lover's caress, heedless of the warning against using his name. "You try to hide it from everyone, but I see it. The darkness. This." She made a gesture with her head indicating his cruel grip and the way he had her pinned. "We're alike, you and I. We need each other. I promise, I'm better suited to you than my perfect, wholesome sister *ever* could be!"

If he'd been given the ages of gods, Rowland Graves would never have expected, even in that span of time, to hear a declaration such as this. He shook his head, attempting to fling the shock away into the night.

"You will *never* be what I need!" His voice broke on those words, the vaulted dome of his reality collapsing in on itself at last. "Oh, God, what have you *done*, you vicious, cursed witch!"

He rolled off her then, hopeless, flopping onto his back, blotting out his vision with a hand over his eyes. His guts were knotting and he wanted to curl himself into a tight bundle against the onslaught of dawning misery.

Elinor!

My angel! What has she done?

What have I done?

The last notion made him want to retch, to claw himself apart.

A cool hand was stroking his face, and a feminine form huddled near.

"Shh, Rowland," the traitor was saying in a sweet voice that had no business issuing from such a foul source. "You will see now. I'll be everything for you. I'll be anything you need me to be. Anything you want."

She'd meant the words to seduce, to quell fear and anger. Instead he shuddered with a laugh that began low under his ribs.

The fissures split wide and light poured in, bloody crimson, queasy yellow, and sinister coiling threads of bile green: goading, throbbing, promising. The wet laugh blossomed into a throaty chuckle and madness embraced Rowland Graves.

Her hand fell away.

"Anything I want?" he asked in a predatory purr, coming up on his elbow again, turning towards her.

"Of course." There was hope in her voice now. "Anything."

In a liquid move, he slid his body back over hers, laying her back down against the earth. Like the impossible lover she seemed to be hoping for, he ran his knuckles down across her cheek. It was at once maddening and heart-wrenching to see the sweet joy in her eyes as he did so.

"Well then," he said to her, "can you be Elinor?"

Her face fell.

"No."

That one word echoed with such hungry, aching sorrow, but Rowland was beyond compassion. He was beyond humanity.

"Then I want you to be *gone*."

Her slender throat was under his fingers. He bore down, putting the deliberate, inevitable weight of his grief into his crushing palm.

At first there was kicking and struggling as she choked and clawed at him with her nails, but the rents in his skin were delicious and he lapped up the pain along with the vision of her widening eyes and the feel of bucking hips.

Doctor Rowland Graves was no stranger to those things that might block an airway. He pressed the first knuckle of his other fist now into the hollow at the base of the frantic throat.

Calm now.

He floated on a smooth sea, detached as he watched her movements reach their delirious, scrambling peak.

And then, Judith Barlow did as he wished for the first and final time.

She was gone.

And so was his soul.

✦

V

DESCENT

The carriage was where he left it, the coachman leaning away from its side, squinting into the night as Rowland returned. The man was smart enough not to abandon his fare, and yet knew better to stay with the horses.

"The lady is not feeling well," he called out as he drew near with a limp female form draped over his arms. "She's had an upset and fainted. We'll need to return to where I left my horse."

The man was quick to open the door for Rowland, but the movements of his limbs betrayed nerves. Another who didn't want to admit a fear of being outdoors on Hallowtide.

"But Doctor Graves," he said, "I could take you straight back to her house. And then I could wait for—"

"I don't intend to keep you out any longer on this night," Rowland said, playing into the man's unspoken superstitions, as he arranged the body on the bench inside the carriage. "Just back to my horse will do. I'll see to the matter from there."

"Sir." The man nodded his acceptance of this, no doubt quite relieved he might no longer be tasked with driving the team straight on through the night.

The carriage bumped and jerked him about as the coachman drove the horses most of the way round a circle to face them in the other direction before setting off back into Bristol proper.

A numb impassivity had settled over him, and his neck and shoulders rolled loose along with the bumping and jostling of carriage wheels, the same as the shell of the woman opposite him did. He said nothing. Thought nothing. All he could to was ride along, waiting to be borne back to the seat of his failure.

<hr />

For a second time since the sun had set, the body of Judith Barlow lay draped behind the saddle of his horse, hidden beneath a blanket. This time, however, it was actually her. Something in his chest constricted at that thought.

The coachman had been easy enough to dismiss, with promises that a medical man had the situation well in hand, and Rowland was now plodding once again towards the cemetery. Just as he'd done earlier, only not the same at all.

He didn't know it yet, but the protective torpor he'd been in since he'd stood in what might have been Earls Mead—if he'd been paying any attention at all at the time—and hoisted the dead woman's body, was a blessing. A blessing which became painfully apparent as he approached the freshly-filled grave for a second time.

At first, the crumbling was nearly unnoticeable. A few grains tumbling down from atop a hill of sand. But as he light from the horse and his shoes neared the edge of the recently-disturbed earth, his knees buckled beneath him. Palms caught his fall, fingers clawing into the soil, and his breath seized in his throat.

Some foreign, rational part of him which existed apart from the utter horror of the moment made him turn his head to the side. He sank his teeth into the meat of his own upper arm and stifled the keening wail that spiralled up and out of him.

No.

No!

No no no no no no nooooooooo!

His eyes came open and he saw the spade leaning where he'd left it. He staggered to his feet and went to snatch it up, returning to thrust it back into the ground against all reason.

Stop, Rowland. You know it's too late. She's gone.

There was no sign from his body that it had heard his mind. The earth flew.

She's gone!

Perhaps the repeated denials that sung in his veins came from some source more essential than mere thought, but either way his muscles, his bones, the sweat now at his brow all disobeyed logic. He wielded the spade with an unnatural fury, carving deeper and faster into the hallowed ground than the drunken sexton ever could.

It must have been well into the wee hours when metal met wood with a hollow thunk. He flung the implement aside at this and went to his hands and knees in the hole, scrabbling what remained of the soil away with raw, desperate, hands.

Rowland was hardly aware of the lid he'd never nailed down as he flipped it aside. He yanked the cloth sack from her head, scraping his knuckles on the coffin wall as he went, and tore at the fox mask, flinging it into the open pit.

Open, pale blue eyes stared back at him, sightless, and he clutched at the too-cold face with both his battered hands. Her once-lovely mouth, the one that called him Love, was slack around the makeshift gag.

You did this, Graves.

This is how his angel had died. Hands and feet bound, sight blinded, wedged bucking and frantic into a narrow box to choke on her own screams until she'd sucked in the last available breath.

You did this to her.

A pointless urgency took him as he fumbled the strap away and plucked the handkerchief from her lips, unable to bear the sight of her that way. Forehead pressed to hers, he tried to catch up her body, hold it to him. The stiffness had already set in, though, and a guttural wail of grief rode out of him as he released her to fall back into the coffin.

"Elinor! Elinor, Elinor, Elinor ..."

Her name came again and again, a mournful incantation, and his fists struck at the wood walls surrounding his only, broken little dove.

Monster.

It was destroyed. Everything. All of it. All of *him*.

Hours might have slid by, or perhaps only minutes. Rowland was no longer functioning within confines that could be explained in those terms. All he knew was that at some point he'd laid a final light, reverent kiss on his angel's brow and, after removing the bonds at her wrists and ankles, he'd replaced the coffin lid and ascended from the grave.

A surge of protective fury lashed out against the idea of burying Elinor's hateful sister in the same place, but there was no time for other plans and nothing to be done for it. With the second body rudely deposited in the hollow with no enclosure of its own, whatever remnants of a man were left that might be piled together and still named Rowland Graves, began filling the hole a final time. Tired didn't matter, nor did empty. The thing must be done, and it was.

He stood there for a time after, blank eyes staring into the night, fingering the scalpel in his coat pocket.

There's another thing that can be done.

The cut would be clean. His pain: ended.

A clean end is too good for you. Monster. You deserve to suffer.

He mounted his horse again, setting off without thought for destination. The grave behind him was a sucking mire, and he only wanted to be away from it.

Somewhere in the fog of events there was another inn, not The Hatchet this time, and there was drink, and then more drink, bought with coin from a purse he'd meant to buy passage on a ship to Amsterdam, a lifetime ago. There were stairs, and stumbling, and a foreign bed to break his fall.

Bone weariness pulled him down, yet some insistent voice didn't want him to sleep. There were monsters in this room.

Just the one.
Angel, I'm sorry.
Oblivion.

⟡

His throat was full of sand, his eyelids swollen. The inside of his skull was a womb of pain. There was light in the room, but not much of it. He'd drifted between sleeping and almost waking for most of the day, and now it seemed to be late afternoon. Or perhaps the ruddy light from the window meant he'd been welcomed to Hell, at last.

With a groan and cough, he rolled onto his back and began a quiet, groggy assessment of himself. At some point he'd managed to get one of his coat sleeves off, but the other still covered an arm and the bulk of the fabric of his coat was rucked up behind him. His shoes were still on, and it didn't seem he'd bothered to make his way under the bed coverings.

There had been knockings at the door, perhaps more than once, but he'd never been awake enough to do anything more about them other than retaining a vague memory of their sound and wishing they would go away.

He swallowed. There had to be water in this room. A pitcher, a washbasin, anything. Blinking again, he let his head fall to the side to look around.

Like lightning, he went from lying prone and stiff to pressing himself in terror into the corner of the room that framed the mattress. His heels scrabbled against the linens in their attempt to push him as far away as possible from the figure waiting for him at the foot of the bed.

Judith Barlow stood smiling at him.

No!

"What in the nine Hells! Be gone, demon!"

He shook his head in an effort to fling away the effects of drink and dreams, but still the viper remained. And now she rose up, impossibly, away from the floor, and in his sudden sobriety he saw her form was not as material as he'd first imagined. Where she began and the room ended was indistinct, and he could now see traces of the walls and door *through* her body.

"Hello, Rowland."

Hair stood up on his arms and the back of his neck, and even his scrotum went tight against his body when the apparition spoke. This was wrong. All wrong.

"Get out!" he croaked, the words rattling in his still-dry throat. "Leave me, ghost! Your time here is ended!" His hands fisted into the pillow and sheet like those of a frightened boy, every muscle tense now, and heart racing. This was impossible.

Abandoning reason, he yanked off one of his shoes and threw it at her. It sailed straight through her body and did nothing to disturb its outline. She laughed in a low, satisfied ripple and the room became cold as a midwinter's day.

"Oh no, my love. My time here has just begun. You took my life on Hallowtide, foolish man. There are no barriers that night between your world and mine. My soul can roam as I wish it now, and as before, I wish for *you*."

The look of triumph in her smile made him shrink

even further into the corner, if that were possible.

"No. No, this is a nightmare! I will awaken! Be gone!" He rubbed at his eyes, willing the spectre before him away, but still she remained.

"What are you?" he demanded. The spirit chuckled at him again.

"I am what remains of Judith Barlow, my fine young doctor. Your own hands caused the death of my body on the Hallowed Eve, and now you are bound to me. My preference would have been to have you while I was alive, but this will do in its stead."

Bound to him?

A thought slapped at him then, and he gave it voice.

"But what of Elinor? Did I not …? That is, is it not my fault that …?" He could not bring himself to say the words.

Monster.

"Oh, no, dear Rowland," the infuriating ghost said, shimmering away from the end of the bed to appear instead directly before him. "Elinor was a good girl. An innocent. There is no haunting and binding for her. Why, I imagine she's singing with the angels at this very moment."

The thing that claimed to be Judith Barlow looked very pleased, but Rowland could not have been more compact in his corner. The last thing he wanted was for the spectre to touch him.

"You're a passionate man," she continued, looking down at him, "I do enjoy that. But it would have been better, had you listened to reason instead while I was still alive. I assure you, I was, and am, more suited to your nature than my sister ever was. I suppose now I have much longer to prove it to you. You will see, in time."

Rowland didn't have the eternal patience the spirit appeared to possess, and saw now she would not leave him, at least not before he had time to discover some means to force her away. In a childish defence against having to look at her, he snatched at the bed sheets and yanked them up over his head, huddling down on his side in the corner.

"Ah, Rowland." He heard her glassy voice still, and a chill line traced over his arm through the sheet, as though the ghost tried to comfort him. "I will hide myself for a time and let you rest, but you'll not be rid of me. And thank you"—she dropped her tone to a mischievous whisper—"for that gift of flesh in the carriage. You were superb, my love. It was no wonder my sister couldn't be persuaded away from you."

He ground his teeth at her final taunt, but as the room grew dark for the evening and he heard no more from the cursed mouth, he managed to uncurl himself and peer out from under the sheet.

The space appeared to be empty. It was also quiet. He must have given over a hefty amount of coin to the innkeep for them to have left him undisturbed for so long.

The foot wearing the stocking alone touched the wood of the floor first, followed by the other, still in its shoe. On wobbly legs he rose and began to feel his way about the darkened room. It was not water, but when his hand closed over the neck of the bottle, he suspected it would be for the best.

He lifted the drink to his lips and hoped it would burn away memory and ghosts the same way it burned down his throat. If Elinor Barlow had gone to Heaven, then it was most certain that Rowland Graves had arrived in Hell.

The bottle clunked to the floor and rolled in half a circle. He was gone again.

Amsterdam, The Netherlands, 1692

"Look there. That one leaving the dressmaker's shop could be made into a fine match for you."

"Go away, Judith," Rowland said under his breath. He moved along the busy market street, ignoring the blonde the disembodied voice had pointed out. She would only appear to him when he was alone, but her voice followed him everywhere.

"Oh, hush. I know what you need, if you'd only listen. She could be your precious Elinor, at the right angle." His fallen angel's name curled from Judith's immaterial tongue like a sneer, and he strode on as if he could outpace it.

He never could.

Ignoring her didn't help either and, to his creeping, exhausted horror, she was beginning to wear at him.

"I was prepared to be anything you wanted, Rowland Graves, but you wouldn't listen."

"And I won't now, either." He kept his eyes forward

"I'll still help you, my love. I'll help you get it all back. Look. Look at her."

With a low growl, he wrenched his head around to see who she was going on about. The young woman was walking in the same direction, on the opposite side of the street, and appeared to be chattering away with what was likely her mother or an aunt.

She did look a bit like Elinor, he admitted to himself. From the side at least. And the way she carried herself, light on her feet, her steps bouncing in the early winter light ...

"Do you see it, Rowland? She's a likely one. She could come to love you, and call your name the way you remember. You only need show her the way. I will help you. And if she's not the one, we'll find some other."

The voice was seductive in his ear, but he ignored it and marched on to his appointment. There was a new doctor in Amsterdam, and he had a reputation to build. He had no time for madness, or spirit voices, or lost loves.

The pain was so very, very real, though, and ever present. Though Judith haunted his steps, it was words between him and Elinor that cut into his core.

I love you, Rowland.

And I love you.

He passed under several more hanging signs from shops and inns, his longing tightly in check. But then his feet were taking him to the other side of the street as all the while his splintering mind denied what he did. Blonde curls under a silk hat bounced in front of him, and Rowland Graves followed, both numb and strangely eager, along behind.

"Yes, Love," Judith purred, *"let me show you."*

The first three or four were failures, each a further gruesome severance of his soul from humanity. He'd been ready to end his own wretched life each time as he saw what he was becoming and fought against it. And each time, Judith was there, picking him up, dusting him off, wiping tears and blood away with her voice.

She would always tell him she loved him, and at first the words were a curling poison in his ears. But these other women never managed to say it, where for Elinor it had been so easy. Effortless. And Judith continued to profess her love, even while, at the very same time, he did unforgivable things. Rowland almost began to believe it was as she said: that no one else could love him but her. Moreover, she pushed him, convinced he could have earthly perfection again if he would only do as she suggested.

He didn't know at what point he gave over the reins, or whether he'd given them over at all or, to his great shame, began agreeing about where his interests lay. Sometimes she appeared to him, and other times only spoke, but the spirit of Judith Barlow had become his only companion, his one guide.

By perhaps the seventh he was no longer afraid. Though it was a stress that he was still convinced none of them would ever be what Judith promised, he found himself beginning to look forward to the challenge.

Amsterdam only lasted a few months, as he was careless in the early days. By the time he left there, however, he had a second trusted companion: Doctor Ellery's scalpel.

Brussels, Orleans, Salzburg ... they all danced by along with months and soon years. Those and more, at Judith's occasional suggestion and his own new drive, which began to build like a cold flame.

They were always blonde, and at first always innocent, though over time these things grew to matter less. Sometimes he would pursue one for months, years even, learning languages and politicking his way into society to be near his current object of pursuit. Other periods would pass where he was impatient and unwilling to go to such measures and would settle for whores: one after another in a rapid, destructive string of flashing medical tools and disappointment.

None of them were ever the One. But their screams and their pleas loved him, for a little while at least, even if he could not make them love him in fact.

And Judith would help him, when he lost his way. It seemed that Rowland Graves lost his way more and more often, these days.

◆

V

The One

✦

Bristol, England, 1716

"You've not taken care of yourself, Brother," Jonathan Graves said as he slid a stack of papers to one side of the massive, polished desk.

Rowland smirked at him from the opposite chair, one ankle resting atop the other knee, his age-worn hands laced together in his lap. He'd seen a mirror. He knew what he looked like.

"The years haven't forgotten *you*, either, Brother." His bite in return was idle, with no true sting in it. Both men wore silver in their hair now, though the man behind the desk had the lion's share.

"Perhaps," the Harbourmaster said, "but at least I have meat on my bones, and a coat that was made some time in this decade. I'm not tripping from port to port, with nowhere to call home."

This list of flaws was true, Rowland allowed, but there were more important things in his dark little world than coats and estates. He inclined his head to his older brother and retained his smile. Insults like these had been passed about between them since they were boys; they didn't rattle him now.

Jonathan pulled one thin sheet of parchment from the rest and pinched it between his fingers, fixing Rowland with a serious glare from across the desk.

"This will be the last time I pluck you away from danger, Little Brother. I thought never to see your face again after that disaster twenty-five years ago."

"Twenty-six," he said in correction. It seemed Rowland could keep track of time when he wanted to, after all.

"Regardless," Jonathan ground on, "I will do this final thing for you, but I assure you it will be the last. Mother and Father are too old for this sort of upset. I won't even be telling them you've been back to Bristol."

"You won't be telling anyone anything." He arched a warning brow at his brother. The only reason Rowland was able to buy this favour at all was that the Harbourmaster of Bristol Port wasn't interested in his contemporaries knowing what sort of things he got up to on his knees in front of the alderman with the ginger hair.

With a grimace, his brother looked back down at the paper, his eyes skimming along. "The captain of *The Devil's Luck* has agreed to take you on as a surgeon," he said, appearing to draw information from whatever it was he read.

"*The Devil's Luck*?" Rowland's eyes glittered. Interesting.

"I see you know the name. Then you also know what sort of men these are, *Doctor* Graves, so I'd suggest you not trifle with them."

"And when does she sail?"

The sooner, the better, he thought, considering one of those whores had managed to wriggle out of his grasp this time.

"I've received word that the ship's here now, and won't be for long, as you might imagine. I suggest you head down the quay and see yourself aboard. Give this to the captain, when you meet him." Jonathan handed him the paper and Rowland folded it and slid it inside his coat without reading.

"My thanks again, Brother," he said, rising from the chair and sketching a mockery of a respectful bow.

The man behind the desk held his gaze with sombre eyes for a long moment. "I don't know what you've become, Brother," he said, "and I don't want to know. But it's time you put this city at your back for good. I expect you never to darken my doorway again."

"And I expect much of the same. By your leave, Brother."

Johnathan Graves tipped him a grim, single nod, and Rowland turned and let himself out of the Harbourmaster's offices into the damp air of the grey morning.

As he stepped out into the street, a blonde woman was emerging from an inn across the crowded avenue with a plump maid in tow. At once, the presence awoke, a stretching beast after a long winter.

Judith was with him again.

"Oooh, Rowland. Look at that one, my love." The long-familiar voice was a caress at his ear. Though he wasn't sure any more whether it was always her when he heard it, or if it might not be a product of what was left of his rational mind after all these years. Either way, he would listen.

He did look, strolling along in the same direction as the pair of women, distracted for the moment from his other goal of finding *The Devil's Luck*.

"She's perfect," Judith chimed away, unseen. *"This is the One, Love, I'm sure of it. If you can only lay hold of her, my dearest, I can feel it. She will be the one who can be what you need. She'll release you from the pain. No more searching and running about, I promise."*

The woman was a fine prize, he allowed that much, but if he wanted her he'd have to separate her from that dour looking maid, or else take them both. And Judith had made such promises so many times before, and none of them ever meant any real end.

"Look at her, Rowland," his ghostly companion said, her

voice persuasive, hungry. *"She only needs but a little guidance from you. A sense of direction."*

He watched the blonde wander in and out of shops, and he followed casually along, the fire of challenge and want kindling low in his belly again. The tilt of her chin and the turn of her wrist were movements in a dance she didn't know she did, stirring him further as he went. Perhaps it was time to stop settling for broken whores in stinking alleys.

Perhaps Judith was right. Maybe this *was* the One.

Yes.

There was a current in the air that made him believe. Some unidentifiable hum. This one could set him free.

"So be it," he muttered, keeping what he hoped would be the last of them in his sights as he walked, "And you'd better be right, Judith, because we'll be at sea for quite some time after today."

The spirit was silent.

"Judith?"

Again, nothing.

Judith Barlow seemed to come and go on a whim, though he wondered, as he often did, whether it was his lost Elinor's sister murmuring in his ear at all, after all this time, or whether it had become his own madness.

No matter. He would guide this little dove himself. She would love him. She would *beg* to love him.

✦

We hope you enjoyed
The Decline and Fall of Rowland Graves!

Like what you read?

Why not leave a review on the site where you purchased your copy? Even a short one is always a great help to independent authors, who rely on readers like you to get the word out about their books.

Ready for more?

Sign up for Eris Adderly's email newsletter:
http://eepurl.com/beYqU1

Get notified about upcoming releases, including:

Books 4 and 5 in *The Skull & Crossbone Romances:*

The Carpenter and the Deckhand
The Merry Widow

Eris only sends emails for new releases (both stories for purchase and free reads), no spam. You can unsubscribe at any time and your address will not be shared.

About Eris

Eris writes dark, escape-from-reality romance full of criminals and outcasts. Expect the decadent and filthy, the crude and sublime, sometimes all at once. She is a complete nerd and possible crazy cat lady. She will annoy you with puns.

Also by Eris Adderly

THE SKULL AND CROSSBONE ROMANCES:

The Devil's Luck – Lust and discovery, betrayal and secrets in the age of sail. Oh yes, and pirates. Dirty, dirty pirates. A young widow from Bristol is ready to sail for the Colonies, but fate seems to have other ideas. A full-length erotic bodice-ripper novel to satisfy your thirst for adventure and pleasure on the high seas.

The Maid and the Cook – A light-hearted, bawdy pirate romance novella following Brigit, the widow's maid from *The Devil's Luck*, and her adventures down in the galley when she catches the unexpected eye of the ship's cook.

AFTER EXILE SERIES

BOOK ONE: *An Emperor for the Eclipse* – A man they call 'exile' and a woman they call 'witch' meet their fate on the steps of the imperial palace. Neither will ever be the same. A dark, romantic fantasy.

FLAMES OF OLYMPOS SERIES

BOOK ONE: *The Eighth House: Hades & Persephone* – The Lord of the Dead must take a wife. Persephone is more than he expects. An erotic, BDSM mythological romance.

BLUSHING BOOKS PUBLICATIONS

Gallows Pole – A notorious highway thief makes a dangerous bargain with a hangman in eighteenth century England. A dark, historical erotic romance novella.

Find Eris Online

www.erisadderly.com
www.facebook.com/erisadderly
www.twitter.com/erisadderly

Printed in Great Britain
by Amazon